TABLE OF CONTENT

Chapter 1: The Enigmatic Light

History and construction of Eilean Mor Lighthouse 1

Its remote location and harsh conditions 2

Chapter 2: The Keepers' Arrival 6

Profiles of the three missing keepers: James Ducat, Thomas Marshall, and Donald MacArthur. 6

Their experience and qualifications 8

Chapter 3: Routine and Isolation 11

The keepers' daily lives at the lighthouse 11

Communication and supply limitations 13

Chapter 4: The Last Days 16

The last known contact with the lighthouse 16

Strange events and communication failures 18

Chapter 5: The Discovery 21

The search and rescue mission 21

The abandoned lighthouse and the missing keepers 23

Chapter 6: Theories and Speculations 26

Theories on what happened to the keepers 26

    Weather-related disasters, attacks, or disappearances 28

Chapter 7: The Investigation 31

    Official inquiries and investigations 31

    Inconsistencies and unanswered questions 33

Chapter 8: The Keepers' Legacy 37

    The impact of their disappearance on their families and the lighthouse community 37

    The haunting mystery surrounding their fate ... 40

Chapter 9: The Weather Factor 43

    Analysis of weather conditions during the disappearance 43

    The role of storms and the lighthouse's vulnerability 45

Chapter 10: The Sea's Fury 49

    The treacherous nature of the surrounding waters 49

    Accounts of other accidents and disappearances 51

Chapter 11: Supernatural Beliefs 53

    Local legends and folklore related to the lighthouse 53

    Theories of ghostly hauntings or other paranormal phenomena 56

Chapter 12: The Unsolved Enigma 59

The ongoing fascination with the case 59

The enduring mystery of the missing keepers ...61

Lessons learned for lighthouse safety and communication 63

Chapter 1: The Enigmatic Lighthouse

History and construction of Eilean Mor Lighthouse

Eilean Mor Lighthouse, perched precariously on a desolate, storm-battered islet off the coast of Scotland, is a testament to human ingenuity in the face of unrelenting nature. Its history, intertwined with the rugged landscape and the relentless forces of the sea, is as fascinating as the enigma of its vanished keepers. .

Construction began in 1899, a response to the treacherous waters surrounding the Flannan Isles, a group of rocky outcroppings notorious for shipwrecks. The need for a lighthouse here was undeniable, but the undertaking was fraught with challenges. The island itself, Eilean Mor, meaning "Big Island" in Gaelic, was a mere speck of land, windswept and unforgiving. Access was only possible in the most favorable weather conditions, requiring skilled seamanship and a hearty dose of courage.

The lighthouse, a marvel of engineering for its time, was built using a combination of local stone and prefabricated iron components. The foundation, laid upon the bedrock of the island, was crucial for withstanding the relentless pounding of the waves. The tower, 37 meters high, was constructed of granite blocks, quarried from the nearby island of Lewis, and meticulously fitted together. The lantern room, crowning the structure, housed the powerful light that would guide ships away from the treacherous shores.

Inside the lighthouse, the keepers' living quarters were spartan but functional. A central living room, a kitchen, and individual bedrooms provided a meager semblance of domesticity. The keepers, isolated from the mainland, relied on a strict routine, tending the powerful lamp, maintaining the station, and keeping a watchful eye on the ever-changing weather. .

The lighthouse, once a beacon of hope against the unforgiving sea, became the stage for a chilling mystery. In December 1900, the three keepers, James Ducat, Thomas Marshall, and Donald MacArthur, vanished without a trace. Their disappearance, shrouded in a cloak of speculation and unanswered questions, has haunted the annals of maritime history.

The construction of Eilean Mor Lighthouse stands as a testament to human ingenuity and the determination to conquer the elements. The structure, despite its harsh location, served as a vital navigational aid, safeguarding countless lives from the treacherous waters. While the mystery of the vanished keepers adds a layer of intrigue to the story, it is the lighthouse itself, a resilient sentinel against the unforgiving forces of nature, that remains the enduring symbol of human endeavor. .

.

Its remote location and harsh conditions

Eilean Mor Lighthouse, a solitary sentinel perched on the rugged coast of the Outer Hebrides, stands as a testament to the unforgiving nature of the North Atlantic. Its remote location, a mere speck in the vast expanse of the ocean, was both its strength and its curse. Isolated on a windswept island, the lighthouse served as a beacon of hope for mariners navigating treacherous waters, yet it also served as a stark reminder of the unforgiving power of the elements.

The island, a rocky outcrop barely larger than a football pitch, was subjected to the full brunt of the Atlantic's fury. Gale-force winds whipped across the exposed landscape, relentlessly battering the lighthouse and its inhabitants. The waves, driven by relentless storms, crashed against the rocky shores with a thunderous roar, their spray reaching high into the air, threatening to engulf the entire island. The isolation was profound, with the nearest mainland settlement a treacherous boat journey away, leaving the lighthouse keepers utterly dependent on the whims of the weather for any communication or resupply.

The very remoteness of Eilean Mor was a factor in the lighthouse's haunting tale. Cut off from the world, the keepers, three men, faced a relentless struggle against the elements. The biting winds pierced through their meager clothing, their skin chapped and raw from constant exposure to the elements. The relentless sea spray permeated everything, leaving a salty tang on their lips and a damp chill that seemed to penetrate their very bones. The island's harsh terrain, covered in sharp rocks and treacherous bogs, added to the challenges they faced, making even the simplest task an ordeal.

The lighthouse, built in the 18th century, stood as a defiant testament to human ingenuity. Yet, the constant struggle against the elements took its toll. The harsh sea air, the relentless spray, and the constant vibration from the lantern's powerful beam slowly eroded the structure. The building, once robust and proud, became worn and weathered, a symbol of the relentless battle against nature. .

The lighthouse's isolation and the harshness of its surroundings were not just physical challenges but also psychological burdens. The relentless storms, the endless expanse of the ocean, and the knowledge of their remoteness created a constant sense of unease and isolation. The keepers, bound by their duty to maintain the light and guide ships to safety, were trapped in a world of their own, with their only companions the wind and the waves.

Life on Eilean Mor was a constant struggle for survival. The men lived in a small, cramped building, with the constant threat of storms looming over them. They were responsible for tending the powerful lantern, a task that demanded unwavering vigilance and precision. The lamp required constant fueling, and the lenses needed meticulous cleaning to ensure the beam shone brightly. The keepers were also responsible for maintaining the machinery, a task that was both challenging and dangerous, given the constant threat of breakdowns and accidents.

The isolation of the lighthouse created a unique set of circumstances. The keepers, cut off from the world and forced to rely on each other, formed a close-knit community. Yet, their isolation also made them vulnerable to the psychological pressures of their surroundings. The constant exposure to the elements, the endless monotony of their daily routine, and the awareness of their isolation could easily lead to feelings of anxiety, depression, and even paranoia.

The harsh conditions of Eilean Mor and the isolation it engendered were central to the mystery of the lighthouse keepers' disappearance. The remoteness of the island made it difficult to ascertain what happened to them. The lack of communication with the mainland, the relentless weather, and the dangers of navigating the treacherous waters all conspired to hinder any investigation. The harshness of the environment also served to amplify the impact of the keepers' disappearance. The lack of human presence on the island only added to the sense of eeriness and mystery that surrounded the event.

The remote location and harsh conditions of Eilean Mor Lighthouse were not just a backdrop to the mystery of the keepers' disappearance, they were integral to it. The isolation, the relentless weather, and the struggle for survival played a crucial role in shaping the lives of the keepers and creating the circumstances that led to their vanishing. The lighthouse, standing as a lonely sentinel against the unforgiving forces of nature, became a symbol of the human struggle against the elements, a struggle that ultimately claimed the lives of three men who dared to face its relentless power.

.

Chapter 2: The Keepers' Arrival

Profiles of the three missing keepers: James Ducat, Thomas Marshall, and Donald MacArthur

The vanishing of James Ducat, Thomas Marshall, and Donald MacArthur from the remote Eilean Mor lighthouse in 1900 remains a baffling mystery. Their disappearance, leaving behind a meticulously maintained lighthouse and a cold, untouched dinner, has captivated the imagination for over a century. Each man brought a unique set of experiences and personalities to the isolated post, their lives intricately woven into the fabric of the lighthouse's history.

James Ducat, the principal keeper, was a seasoned mariner with a meticulous nature. His meticulous journal entries, detailing the lighthouse's operation and weather conditions, provide a haunting glimpse into the final days before the disappearance. Ducat's disciplined approach and unwavering commitment to duty are evident throughout his recordings, highlighting his steadfastness and dedication to his role. His careful attention to detail, evident in both his work and personal life, suggests a man deeply invested in maintaining order and routine. The meticulous nature of his last entries adds an unsettling layer to the mystery, painting a portrait of a man who meticulously documented his final days, seemingly oblivious to the unsettling events that were soon to unfold.

Thomas Marshall, the assistant keeper, was a man of quiet reserve, known for his stoic demeanor and unwavering dependability. He was a skilled seaman, accustomed to life at sea, and his presence likely provided a sense of calm and stability within the small lighthouse community. Marshall's quiet nature, in contrast to Ducat's methodical approach, suggests a different temperament, yet one that contributed to the efficient functioning of the lighthouse. His disappearance, leaving behind a half-finished knitting project, hints at a sudden and unforeseen event, disrupting his everyday routine. The unfinished task speaks to a life abruptly halted, leaving behind a poignant reminder of the ordinary moments that were forever disrupted.

Donald MacArthur, the youngest of the three keepers, was a man of youthful exuberance and boundless energy. While his experience at sea was limited compared to his colleagues, his eagerness to learn and contribute to the lighthouse's operation made him a valuable asset. His enthusiasm and optimistic spirit likely provided a welcome counterpoint to the somber atmosphere of the isolated island. MacArthur's youthful energy, a stark contrast to Ducat's age and experience, provides a dimension of hope and possibility within the otherwise austere environment. The sudden absence of his youthful vitality, leaving behind a half-eaten meal, adds a jarring note to the story, highlighting the abrupt and unexpected nature of their disappearance.

The contrasting personalities of James Ducat, Thomas Marshall, and Donald MacArthur, each with their unique skills and contributions, reveal the intricate tapestry of lives woven together within the isolated Eilean Mor lighthouse. Their disappearance, leaving behind a meticulously maintained beacon of light and a haunting sense of stillness, has left behind a legacy of unanswered questions, captivating generations with the enigma of their vanishing. Their stories, forever intertwined with the fate of the lighthouse, stand as a chilling testament to the unpredictability of life and the enduring mystery of their disappearance. .

.

Their experience and qualifications

The chilling tale of Eilean Mor Lighthouse and the vanishing keepers, Joseph Moore, James Ducat, and Donald MacArthur, hinges on the experience and qualifications of these men, who were entrusted with the vital task of maintaining the light that guided ships through the treacherous waters off the coast of Scotland.

Joseph Moore, the principal keeper, was a seasoned veteran with 17 years of experience in the lighthouse service. Having served on various stations along the rugged Scottish coastline, he was well-versed in the challenges posed by the unforgiving sea. His expertise in lighthouse operation and maintenance was unquestionable, and he was undoubtedly the most experienced of the three keepers. .

James Ducat, the second keeper, had a comparatively shorter tenure in the service, having joined only two years prior to the disappearance. However, he had already served at several stations, including Eilean Mor. Ducat's experience, though less extensive than Moore's, still placed him within the realm of competent and qualified keepers, capable of operating and maintaining the lighthouse effectively.

Donald MacArthur, the youngest of the three, joined the lighthouse service only months before the disappearance, making him the least experienced. While his knowledge of lighthouse operations was undoubtedly limited, his youthful energy and eagerness to learn made him a valuable addition to the crew. .

The qualifications of these keepers were essential to their duties. The lighthouse service rigorously trained individuals in the art of lighthouse maintenance, ensuring that they were equipped with the necessary skills to operate complex optical equipment, maintain the lantern and its fuel supply, and keep meticulous records of their work. .

The keepers' experiences varied, but each one brought a unique set of skills and knowledge to the team. Joseph Moore's seasoned experience was invaluable, while James Ducat provided a balance of experience and youth, and Donald MacArthur represented the potential for future success in the lighthouse service. Their collective experience and qualifications represented the necessary skillset to ensure the safe and effective operation of Eilean Mor Lighthouse. .

It is crucial to understand that these were not simply ordinary men assigned to a remote outpost. They were chosen for their skills and experience, and entrusted with a vital responsibility that directly impacted the safety of countless lives. Their disappearance under mysterious circumstances, leaving no explanation, and only a few ambiguous clues, underscores the importance of the experience and qualifications these men possessed, making their fate all the more perplexing and unsettling. .

.

Chapter 3: Routine and Isolation

The keepers' daily lives at the lighthouse

The daily routine of the keepers at Eilean Mor Lighthouse was a symphony of precise timing and meticulous execution, a testament to the demanding nature of their isolated existence. Their lives were bound to the rhythm of the sea, the ever-present hum of the foghorn, and the unwavering responsibility of maintaining the light that guided mariners through the treacherous waters. .

Each day began at the crack of dawn, the keepers rising to a chorus of seagulls and the rhythmic crashing of waves against the craggy rocks. The first order of business was to tend to the lighthouse itself, meticulously cleaning the powerful lens and ensuring its pristine condition. This task was not merely about aesthetics; it was a crucial element in guaranteeing the efficient operation of the light, a beacon of safety for ships navigating the treacherous waters surrounding the island. .

The keepers' days were punctuated by a series of meticulously planned tasks. The lantern required constant attention, its oil reservoir replenished, the wick trimmed, and the lamp meticulously adjusted. The foghorn, a mechanical marvel of the time, needed regular servicing and careful operation, its mournful calls echoing across the desolate landscape. The keepers would carefully monitor the weather, recording wind speed and direction, the intensity of the sea, and the ever-changing conditions of the treacherous currents. These meticulously documented observations were essential for understanding the island's volatile environment and predicting potential dangers for mariners. .

In the absence of modern communication technology, the keepers relied on a system of meticulously crafted signals to communicate with the mainland. They would use semaphore flags, a rudimentary but effective means of conveying messages across the vast stretches of sea. These signals, often meticulously crafted to convey specific information, were their lifeline to the outside world, allowing them to request supplies, report weather conditions, and ensure their safety in the face of emergencies. .

While their primary duty was the lighthouse, the keepers' responsibilities extended to other aspects of life on the remote island. They meticulously tended to their small garden, cultivating vegetables to supplement their rations. They would collect rainwater, their only source of fresh water, ensuring a constant supply for their needs. And during their downtime, they would engage in various activities, from reading books and playing games to meticulously documenting their experiences and observations. .

The keepers' lives at Eilean Mor were a study in self-reliance and resilience. They lived with an awareness of the power of the sea and the constant threat of isolation. Yet, within these constraints, they developed a unique bond, a camaraderie forged in the crucible of shared responsibility and the constant presence of the relentless sea. .

Their daily lives were a testament to their dedication to their duties, their ability to thrive in the most challenging conditions, and their deep connection to the unforgiving beauty of the island they called home. Their lives were marked by a stark simplicity, a focus on the essentials, and a profound respect for the power of nature. They were the guardians of the light, their dedication a testament to the silent heroism of those who serve as sentinels in the face of the unforgiving forces of the sea. .

.

Communication and supply limitations

The isolation of Eilean Mor Lighthouse, a remote outpost perched on a windswept Scottish island, played a pivotal role in the disappearance of its keepers in 1900. The very nature of the lighthouse's location, far from any mainland settlement and accessible only by treacherous boat journey, rendered it a virtual prison of isolation. This inherent remoteness imposed significant constraints on communication and supply, creating a perfect storm of vulnerability for the keepers.

The primary communication lifeline for the lighthouse keepers was the Morse code telegraph, a system that relied on the whims of the weather. The telegram's effectiveness was directly proportional to the clarity of the signal, a factor heavily influenced by atmospheric conditions. Storms, fog, and heavy seas could easily disrupt the telegraph's operation, effectively cutting off communication with the mainland. In a place where darkness reigned for much of the year, reliance on this technology for routine communication became a risky proposition.

Beyond the telegram, the lighthouse keepers were reliant on infrequent boat visits for supplies. The perilous journey across the treacherous waters around Eilean Mor was undertaken only when conditions allowed, a precarious balance between necessity and the mercy of the sea. This irregular supply schedule left the keepers vulnerable to unexpected delays and shortages, forcing them to rely on their limited reserves and ingenuity to manage.

The lack of regular communication and supply lines, a consequence of the lighthouse's isolation, created a profound sense of vulnerability for the keepers. They were effectively cut off from the outside world, their fate hanging in the balance of nature's whims. This constant state of precariousness, where communication could be disrupted and supplies could run out, created a palpable tension that permeated their lives.

Furthermore, the isolation of the lighthouse fostered an atmosphere of dependence and reliance on the immediate group. The keepers were a small community unto themselves, forced to rely on each other for companionship, support, and even survival. In the absence of regular contact with the outside world, their interactions with each other became paramount, creating a close-knit bond but also highlighting the potential consequences of internal conflict or mistrust.

The isolation of Eilean Mor Lighthouse, therefore, served as a catalyst for the communication and supply limitations that plagued the keepers. This isolation was not merely a geographical reality but a defining aspect of their lives, profoundly impacting their daily routine, their sense of vulnerability, and ultimately their fate. It is this very isolation, in its various forms, that serves as the foundation of the mystery surrounding the disappearance of the lighthouse keepers, a story forever etched in the annals of maritime lore. . .

Chapter 4: The Last Days

The last known contact with the lighthouse

The last known contact with the Eilean Mor lighthouse keepers, Thomas Marshall, James Ducat, and Donald McArthur, occurred on December 15, 1900. The communication was a simple, routine signal - a flash of light from the lighthouse lantern. This solitary signal, a flicker across the churning North Atlantic, was the final message received from the island, a message devoid of any hint of the tragedy unfolding within the lighthouse walls. The signal, sent at the precise time it should have been, was misinterpreted as a sign of normalcy, a continuation of the meticulous routine that governed the lives of the keepers. The lighthouse was functioning flawlessly, the light flashing as it should. But this ordinary, mechanical flash of light would become a chilling testament to the unseen horror that had already claimed the lives of the keepers, the last, silent echo of a life tragically extinguished.

The signal, a fleeting beam in the vast expanse of the ocean, was observed by the passing steamer, the "Hesperus." This vessel, itself a testament to the human drive to conquer the sea, unknowingly bore witness to the final act of the lighthouse drama. The "Hesperus" was not a scheduled visitor to Eilean Mor. Its presence, a chance encounter in the vast ocean, was a fleeting moment of connection, a moment that, despite its briefness, would become a crucial piece in the puzzle of the lighthouse's haunting disappearance. The steamer's captain, likely unaware of the impending tragedy, would later provide a vital piece of information, confirming that the lighthouse's signal was functioning as normal on December 15, 1900. This routine observation, a simple note in the captain's log, would later become a haunting reminder of the last known contact with the keepers, a tragic confirmation that the lighthouse's light, while functioning flawlessly, was no longer guided by the hands of the men who had been its sole keepers.

The subsequent weeks and months would see the silence of the lighthouse grow heavier, punctuated only by the unanswered calls of the lighthouse inspector, Joseph Moore. The absence of a response to Moore's calls, the lack of the expected, routine signals, would slowly unveil the chilling truth: The lighthouse, though functioning mechanically, had fallen silent. The light, a beacon of hope and safety, had become a symbol of the tragedy that had unfolded, its steady, unwavering beam now casting an eerie glow over the isolated island, a silent testament to the disappearance of its keepers. .

The routine signal, a simple flash of light, had served its purpose. It was the last known contact, a mechanical whisper across the vast ocean, a final, fleeting moment of connection with the three men who had entrusted their lives to the isolated lighthouse. The lighthouse, a silent sentinel, would continue to perform its duty, its unwavering light a reminder of the tragedy that had unfolded within its walls, a silent tribute to the vanished keepers of Eilean Mor. .

Strange events and communication failures

The narrative begins with a chilling account of the final message sent by James Ducat, the principal keeper, on December 15, 1900. The cryptic telegram, "All well," is a stark contrast to the later discovery of the keepers' absence and the eerie silence that engulfed Eilean Mor. The message itself, while seemingly innocuous, becomes a chilling premonition in hindsight, raising questions about the true state of affairs on the island. .

Adding to the unsettling atmosphere are the accounts of the local villagers who reported seeing strange lights emanating from the lighthouse in the days leading up to the disappearance. These sightings, coupled with the absence of any response to repeated attempts at communication, create an unsettling sense of unease and hint at an underlying mystery.

The communication failures play a crucial role in escalating the sense of dread and confusion surrounding the disappearance. The lighthouse, despite its strategic importance and its crucial role in ensuring safe maritime navigation, was tragically isolated and lacked reliable communication systems. The reliance on unreliable telegraphy, hampered by inclement weather and technical difficulties, proved to be a significant obstacle in establishing contact with the keepers. .

The absence of any response to telegrams, the unanswered calls for assistance, and the futile attempts to reach the island by sea highlight the tragic limitations of technology in a time when communication was a lifeline, not a given. This communication void, combined with the lack of any clear explanation for the keepers' disappearance, fuels speculation and fuels the fire of fear.

The narrative further emphasizes the haunting nature of the disappearance through the descriptions of the keepers' living quarters and the unsettling discovery of their belongings. The meticulously kept notebooks, the untouched personal items, and the presence of food provisions, all speak of a sudden and unexpected departure, leaving behind a sense of unsettling normalcy amidst the eerie silence.

These details, coupled with the chilling account of the boat found washed ashore with its oars still locked in place, paint a picture of a sudden and inexplicable departure, suggesting a mysterious force at play. The eerie stillness of the island, the lack of any signs of struggle or conflict, and the presence of unfinished tasks all contribute to the unsettling sense of mystery surrounding the keepers' disappearance.

The chapter culminates with the arrival of the relief vessel, the "Hesperus," and the chilling discovery of the keepers' absence. The sense of dread and uncertainty that pervades the narrative is further amplified by the discovery of the lighthouse's malfunctioning lantern, adding another layer of mystery and emphasizing the urgent need to find out what transpired on Eilean Mor. .

The strange events, the communication failures, and the inexplicable circumstances all converge to paint a picture of an unsettling and haunting enigma. It is this meticulously crafted narrative, steeped in mystery and suspense, that captivates the reader's imagination and compels them to delve deeper into the depths of this enigmatic case.

.

Chapter 5: The Discovery

The search and rescue mission

The chilling disappearance of the three lighthouse keepers, James Ducat, Thomas Marshall, and Donald MacArthur, from the remote Eilean Mor lighthouse in 1900 triggered a desperate search and rescue mission. The mission, fraught with challenges presented by the island's isolation and the harsh weather conditions, reflected the Victorian era's commitment to maritime safety and the human cost of duty. .

The initial reports of the missing men reached the mainland on December 15th, 1900, sparking immediate action. The news, relayed by the passing steamer "Archtor," triggered a flurry of activity, with the authorities immediately realizing the urgency of the situation. The remoteness of Eilean Mor, situated on a small island off the coast of the Outer Hebrides, posed the first major obstacle. Reaching the island, especially during the harsh winter months, was no easy feat, requiring skilled seamanship and luck with the weather. .

The search and rescue effort was spearheaded by the Board of Trade, which dispatched a lifeboat from Stornoway, the nearest port. The lifeboat, "The Stornoway," was a formidable vessel, capable of navigating treacherous waters, but the journey to Eilean Mor was still perilous. The crew, brave and experienced, braved the raging waves and unpredictable currents, highlighting the risks involved in the rescue operation. .

The search itself was a grueling endeavor, hampered by the harsh conditions and the limited resources available. The search party, consisting of experienced seamen and local islanders, scoured the island's rugged terrain, braving the icy winds and the unforgiving landscape. The relentless search continued, fueled by hope and a sense of duty, despite the growing sense of unease about the missing men's fate. .

The island's topography further complicated the search. Its rocky cliffs and treacherous coastline made access difficult, demanding meticulous search patterns. Despite the challenges, the rescue team persevered, combing every inch of the island, meticulously checking every possible hiding place, every crevice, and every cave. Each day, the hope of finding the missing men dwindled, replaced by a creeping sense of dread.

The weather played a significant role in shaping the search. The unforgiving winter storms, characteristic of the Hebrides, made navigation treacherous and hampered visibility. The relentless winds and heavy seas tested the mettle of the search party, making their task even more challenging. They battled the elements, enduring the freezing temperatures and the constant threat of being swept away by the unforgiving waves.

The search party discovered evidence of a struggle, further fueling the mystery surrounding the disappearance. The discovery of a single boot, seemingly thrown against the rocks, added a chilling layer of mystery to the unfolding events. The search continued, but the relentless storms and the island's unforgiving terrain took their toll. The rescue mission, initially hopeful, slowly transformed into a search for the missing men's remains, a somber acknowledgment of the tragic reality. .

The search ultimately proved unsuccessful. No trace of the lighthouse keepers was ever found, and the mystery of their disappearance remains unsolved to this day. The search and rescue mission, a testament to human resilience and the spirit of community, ended with a heavy heart, leaving behind a lingering sense of unease and a haunting reminder of the unforgiving nature of the sea. .

.

The abandoned lighthouse and the missing keepers

The Eilean Mor Lighthouse, perched precariously on a windswept island off the coast of Scotland, stands as a stark testament to a chilling mystery. Built in 1899, the lighthouse was designed to guide ships through the treacherous waters surrounding the island, its beams a beacon of hope for mariners navigating the turbulent North Atlantic. However, the Eilean Mor lighthouse is far more than a beacon of safety. Its history is intertwined with the haunting disappearance of three lighthouse keepers, a mystery that has captivated and baffled the world for over a century. .

The story begins in December 1900. The keepers, Thomas Marshall, James Ducat, and Donald MacArthur, were last seen alive on December 15th.

Their families, expecting a routine communication from their loved ones, were met with silence. The lighthouse, despite its strategic importance, was not equipped with radio communication, relying solely on the keepers' diligence in manually transmitting messages. The lack of any contact sparked alarm, and a search party was swiftly dispatched to the remote island.

What they found was a scene of utter desolation. The lighthouse, seemingly abandoned, stood silent, its lamp extinguished. The keepers' quarters were in disarray, with their belongings scattered throughout the rooms, as if they had departed in haste. The lighthouse log, meticulously maintained, ended abruptly on December 15th, with no mention of any unusual events. The only sign of any struggle was a partially eaten meal found in the kitchen, hinting at a sudden departure. .

The official investigation, conducted by the Northern Lighthouse Board, concluded that the keepers had likely been swept away by a rogue wave, their bodies lost to the unforgiving sea. The disappearance was attributed to the harsh and unpredictable nature of the Atlantic, a common occurrence in the region. However, many unanswered questions remain. .

The lack of any physical evidence, like washed-up debris or the keepers' bodies, is a primary point of contention. The meticulously kept log, ending abruptly without any indication of distress, raises further suspicion. The scattered belongings within the keepers' quarters also point towards a hurried departure, but without any indication of an external threat, suggesting a scenario far more sinister than a natural disaster. .

The Eilean Mor lighthouse has become a place of whispered tales and speculation. Theories abound, ranging from pirate attacks to supernatural phenomena. Some believe that the keepers succumbed to a strange illness, perhaps a combination of isolation and psychological distress. Others suggest that the keepers, driven by an unknown fear, abandoned the lighthouse, never to be seen again. .

The mystery of the Eilean Mor lighthouse remains unresolved. The abandoned structure, a testament to the unpredictable nature of the sea and the enduring mystery of human disappearance, continues to captivate the imagination. The lighthouse, a beacon of light in the darkness, serves as a stark reminder of the enduring power of the unknown, the chilling possibilities that lie hidden beneath the surface of reality.

Chapter 6: Theories and Speculations

Theories on what happened to the keepers

The disappearance of the three keepers of Eilean Mor Lighthouse in 1900 remains a haunting enigma, fueling endless speculation and theories. The absence of any concrete evidence, coupled with the isolation and harsh conditions of the island, has given rise to a plethora of explanations, ranging from the mundane to the extraordinary. .

One prominent theory suggests that the disappearance was the result of a severe storm. The island is known for its volatile weather, and a particularly violent storm could have engulfed the lighthouse, sweeping the keepers away. This theory draws support from the fact that the lighthouse's lantern was extinguished during the period of their disappearance, potentially due to storm damage. However, this explanation fails to account for the absence of any debris or bodies washing ashore, which would be expected in the event of a fatal storm. .

Another theory posits that the keepers may have succumbed to accidental death, possibly due to a fall from the cliff edges or a mishap during routine maintenance. The lighthouse itself is situated on a rocky and precarious outcrop, making accidental falls a plausible scenario. However, the absence of any signs of a struggle or any evidence of a fall makes this explanation less convincing.

The possibility of foul play, either at the hands of a third party or through an act of internal conflict, has also been explored. This theory suggests that a conflict may have arisen between the keepers, leading to a violent confrontation. The possibility of a disgruntled individual seeking revenge cannot be ruled out either. However, there is no evidence to suggest any prior animosity or disputes between the keepers, rendering this theory less likely.

A more intriguing possibility is that the keepers were victims of a maritime disaster. They may have been caught in a rogue wave or been struck by a ship, swept away into the sea, leaving no trace. The isolation of the island makes this scenario plausible, as there would be no witnesses to the event. .

The most outlandish theory, and perhaps the one that has captured the public imagination the most, is the possibility of paranormal activity. Some speculate that the lighthouse was haunted by a malevolent entity that lured the keepers to their demise. This theory gains credence from the eerie nature of the disappearance, the unsettling descriptions of the island by locals, and the lack of any logical explanation.

The disappearance of the keepers of Eilean Mor Lighthouse remains an unresolved mystery. While the absence of evidence makes it difficult to definitively pinpoint the cause, the theories discussed provide a glimpse into the various possibilities and the enduring fascination surrounding this enigmatic event. The mystery continues to tantalize and intrigue, serving as a stark reminder of the power of nature, the dangers of isolation, and the enduring allure of the unknown. . .

Weather-related disasters, attacks, or disappearances

The disappearance of the three lighthouse keepers from Eilean Mor in 1900 remains shrouded in mystery, and weather-related events loom large in the tapestry of theories surrounding their fate. The island's harsh and unforgiving environment, characterized by relentless gales, treacherous seas, and unpredictable fog, provided a formidable backdrop for the tragedy. The very nature of their isolation, their reliance on the unforgiving whims of the sea and weather, only amplified the sense of mystery surrounding their disappearance.

One prevalent theory suggests that a storm of exceptional ferocity struck the island, sweeping the men away in a violent torrent of wind and rain. The lighthouse itself, perched precariously on a rocky islet, was particularly vulnerable to the full fury of Atlantic storms. While the official inquiry ruled out any evidence of a storm during the time of their disappearance, historical records reveal the possibility of a rogue wave. These colossal waves, appearing suddenly and unpredictably, can reach staggering heights, capable of crashing over sea walls and engulfing entire ships. The relentless onslaught of such a wave, especially on the exposed island, could have easily overpowered the lighthouse keepers and washed them away into the unforgiving depths.

The possibility of a powerful storm, coupled with the lighthouse's exposed location, presents a compelling narrative for the keepers' disappearance. The treacherous conditions, coupled with the inherent isolation of their post, could have rendered the men helpless in the face of nature's wrath. The harsh reality of the weather, in its unpredictable and powerful form, could have played a devastating role in their fate. .

Another facet of the weather-related theories focuses on the impact of dense fog on the island. Thick blankets of fog, an endemic characteristic of the Scottish coast, could have enveloped the island, obscuring the lighthouse and hindering any attempts at rescue. The dense fog could have effectively cut the keepers off from the mainland, isolating them further and contributing to their disappearance. The fog, in its ability to erase visibility and disorient even the most seasoned mariner, could have played a decisive role in the tragedy.

However, the absence of any evidence of a storm in the official inquiry and the absence of any signs of struggle on the island raise questions about the veracity of this theory. The absence of any wreckage or debris from the lighthouse or the keepers further fuels the mystery. The lack of any direct evidence of a storm or any indication of a struggle suggests that the keepers may have met their end in a less dramatic and more insidious way. .

It is crucial to acknowledge that the absence of evidence does not necessarily disprove the weather-related theories entirely. The ferocity of the Atlantic, the island's isolation, and the unpredictability of the weather conditions all contribute to the plausibility of a weather-related disaster. The enduring mystery of Eilean Mor reinforces the power of nature and its ability to reshape lives and stories in its own enigmatic fashion. .

The enigma surrounding the disappearance of the lighthouse keepers remains unsolved, leaving a void filled with speculation and conjecture. The weather, in its raw and unforgiving power, continues to loom large in the narrative, serving as both a potential catalyst and a formidable obstacle to the resolution of the mystery. The lack of concrete evidence, however, compels us to consider alternative explanations for their disappearance, reminding us of the complex interplay of human fate and the whims of nature. .

Chapter 7: The Investigation

Official inquiries and investigations

The disappearance of the three keepers from Eilean Mor lighthouse in 1900, Thomas Marshall, James Ducat, and Donald MacArthur, sent shockwaves through the maritime community and triggered an official inquiry that sought to unravel the mystery behind their vanishing. The investigation, undertaken by the Northern Lighthouse Board (NLB), was a painstaking process that involved meticulous examination of the lighthouse, its surrounding environment, and any available evidence.

The first step in the investigation involved a thorough inspection of the lighthouse and its immediate surroundings. The NLB deployed a team of experienced lighthouse engineers and inspectors to conduct a comprehensive search. This involved examining the lighthouse's machinery, its lighting system, and all the structures within the compound. The investigators scrutinized the logs, journals, and any other records kept by the keepers, seeking any clues or inconsistencies that might shed light on their disappearance.

The NLB team carefully examined the lighthouse's location and its accessibility. They considered the weather conditions prevailing at the time of the disappearance, the state of the sea, and the potential for any external events that could have impacted the lighthouse or its occupants. They also investigated the possibility of any external threats, including storms, shipwrecks, or hostile encounters with passing vessels.

The investigators interviewed the keepers' families and acquaintances, gathering information about their personal lives, relationships, and any potential financial or personal problems that might have driven them to leave the lighthouse. They also reached out to local fishermen and people who had been in contact with the lighthouse keepers, seeking any reports or observations about their behavior in the days leading up to their disappearance. .

The NLB also contacted the local police and the coastguard, requesting any information or reports that might be related to the disappearance. They investigated any sightings of the lighthouse keepers or their boat in the surrounding waters and sought information about any potential incidents that might have occurred near the lighthouse during that period.

As the investigation progressed, the NLB faced several challenges. The remoteness of the lighthouse made access difficult, hindering communication and limiting the scope of the search. The lack of modern communication technologies at the time also posed a significant obstacle, delaying the dissemination of information and limiting the effectiveness of the investigation. .

The investigation ultimately concluded that the disappearance of the keepers was a mystery with no concrete explanation. The NLB ruled out any foul play or external factors that might have caused the disappearance. Their investigation also found no evidence of any internal conflict, financial issues, or personal problems that would have motivated the keepers to leave the lighthouse willingly.

The NLB investigation was unable to pinpoint the precise reason for the disappearance. The investigation generated multiple theories, ranging from a rogue wave to a fatal accident at sea. However, none of these theories could be conclusively proven. The case of the vanishing keepers of Eilean Mor lighthouse, therefore, remained an unsolved mystery, adding to the intrigue surrounding the incident.

The NLB investigation was a significant undertaking that employed various methods to uncover the truth behind the disappearance. While it failed to provide a definitive answer, it meticulously ruled out various possibilities and generated valuable insights into the circumstances surrounding the incident. .

The lack of a conclusive explanation fueled speculation and fuelled the public's fascination with the mystery. The case of the vanishing keepers of Eilean Mor lighthouse became a subject of countless books, articles, and documentaries, captivating generations with its enduring enigma.

.

Inconsistencies and unanswered questions

The chapter titled "The Investigation" in the narrative of the Eilean Mor lighthouse tragedy presents a seemingly meticulous account of the official inquiry into the disappearance of the three keepers.

Firstly, the speed and apparent ease with which the investigation was conducted raises eyebrows. Despite the remote location and the severity of the situation, the official inquiry was completed remarkably quickly. The initial visit to the lighthouse, the examination of the scene, and the subsequent interviews with the islanders all transpired within a short period, leaving little time for thorough analysis and exploration of potential alternative explanations.

Furthermore, the official report relies heavily on assumptions and circumstantial evidence, leaving crucial questions unanswered. For instance, the absence of any signs of a struggle or forced entry is presented as evidence that the keepers willingly left the lighthouse. The lack of any evidence regarding the whereabouts of the keepers' personal belongings, particularly their personal effects and navigational tools, further fuels the mystery and begs for further investigation.

The official narrative conveniently ignores the reports of unusual activity around the lighthouse prior to the disappearance. Local islanders, particularly those who frequented the lighthouse for supplies, reported seeing strange lights and hearing noises that were out of place. These reports, dismissed as mere superstition by the investigating officers, could hold vital clues to the true events that transpired. Their exclusion from the official report raises questions about the comprehensiveness and objectivity of the investigation.

The chapter also raises concerns about the handling of evidence, or rather, the lack thereof. While the official report states that the search for the keepers was extensive, the details of the search efforts remain vague. Notably, the extent of the search on and around the island, the specific areas explored, and the methods employed are not clearly documented. The absence of a detailed account of the search procedure leaves room for speculation about the thoroughness and effectiveness of the investigation.

Perhaps the most baffling inconsistency lies in the lack of any investigation into the possibility of foul play. Despite the circumstances surrounding the disappearance and the reported unusual activity, the investigators appear to have dismissed the possibility of a criminal act without any concrete evidence to support their assumption. This lack of investigation into a potential external factor, coupled with the emphasis on the keepers' supposed "willing departure," leaves a significant gap in the official narrative.

Ultimately, the "Investigation" chapter, while presenting a seemingly comprehensive account of the official inquiry, fails to adequately address the complexities of the Eilean Mor mystery. The numerous inconsistencies and unanswered questions raise serious doubts about the thoroughness and objectivity of the investigation, leaving the public to grapple with a case that remains shrouded in uncertainty. The unresolved questions and the lack of a conclusive explanation continue to fuel speculation and intrigue, ensuring that the haunting tale of the

Eilean Mor lighthouse keepers will continue to captivate and mystify generations to come.

Chapter 8: The Keepers' Legacy

The impact of their disappearance on their families and the lighthouse community

The disappearance of James Ducat, Thomas Marshall, and Donald MacArthur, the three keepers of Eilean Mor Lighthouse, ripped a gaping hole in the hearts of their families and the tight-knit community of lighthouse workers. The immediate shock and disbelief were soon overtaken by a gut-wrenching fear that gnawed at their souls. The men were beacons of reliability, their absence a jarring reminder of the unpredictable nature of the sea and the isolating remoteness of their duty. Their families were plunged into a labyrinth of grief, the hope of their return slowly dwindling with each passing day. Their wives, accustomed to the quiet routine of life on the mainland, were now left to navigate the treacherous tides of uncertainty alone. The weight of their husbands' absence, the unanswered questions, the whispers of rumors, and the relentless news reports conspired to create a suffocating atmosphere of despair. .

The children, innocent to the complexities of their fathers' fate, were left to grapple with their absence in their own ways. Their childhood innocence was prematurely shattered, replaced by a haunting silence that echoed the missing voices of their fathers. The community, bound by the shared experiences of life at sea, felt the loss as if it were their own. They mourned the loss of their colleagues, their neighbors, their friends. The disappearance cast a shadow of fear over the lighthouse community, shattering their sense of security and forever changing their perception of the treacherous waters that surrounded them. Their work, once a source of pride and purpose, was now tainted with a sense of dread. The men's absence served as a stark reminder of the constant danger inherent in their profession, a danger that could swallow a man whole, leaving behind only whispers of his existence. .

The community rallied around the families, offering their support and solace. They shared meals, offered childcare, and provided companionship, attempting to ease the burden of grief that weighed heavy on their hearts. Yet, the gaping hole left by the missing keepers remained, an unhealed wound that continued to bleed. The families, caught in a web of unanswered questions, faced an uphill battle to rebuild their lives. The missing men became part of their everyday lives, their absence a constant ache that time could not soothe. The community, forever marked by the disappearance, became more vigilant, more cautious, and more united. The bond that united them, forged in the harsh realities of their profession, was strengthened by the shared experience of their loss. The disappearance of the keepers served as a cautionary tale, a chilling reminder of the power of the sea and the fragility of human life in the face of its wrath. .

The absence of the three men had a profound impact on the Scottish lighthouse community. The whispers of their disappearance resonated throughout the network, a chilling reminder of the dangers that lurked beneath the surface of the seemingly calm waters. The sense of vulnerability, once a hushed concern, now became a palpable fear, a constant presence in the daily lives of the lighthouse keepers. The lighthouse, a symbol of hope and safety, became a haunted reminder of their vulnerability. Every shift, every storm, every sunset, was a reminder of the men who had vanished without a trace. The fear, the uncertainty, and the shared grief forged an unbreakable bond within the community, a bond that served as a testament to the resilience of human spirit in the face of loss. .

The families, left behind to navigate the turbulent seas of grief, found solace in each other's company. They shared their stories, their fears, and their hopes, finding strength in their shared sorrow. The community became their extended family, offering support and a sense of belonging in a world that had suddenly become unfamiliar and unforgiving. The loss of the keepers became a shared experience, a reminder of the fragility of life and the importance of community in times of hardship. .

The disappearance of the three keepers from Eilean Mor Lighthouse became a haunting reminder of the mysteries that lay beneath the surface of the sea, the power of nature, and the enduring legacy of human loss. It forever changed the lives of their families, the lighthouse community, and the annals of Scottish history. Their story, a testament to the resilience and the fragility of the human spirit, continues to resonate with a chilling urgency, a reminder of the enduring mystery that surrounds the disappearance of the keepers of Eilean Mor. .

The haunting mystery surrounding their fate

The haunting mystery surrounding the fate of the three lighthouse keepers on Eilean Mor, a remote island off the coast of Scotland, remains an enduring enigma, drawing the attention of historians, researchers, and enthusiasts alike. The disappearance of James Ducat, Thomas Marshall, and Donald McArthur in December 1900 under such peculiar circumstances has left behind a trail of unanswered questions, feeding a fertile ground for speculation and theories. The lack of a definitive explanation for their vanishing has cemented the incident as a chilling and enduring mystery.

The official accounts of the events paint a stark and unsettling picture. On December 15, 1900, the supply steamer, the "Hesperus," arrived at Eilean Mor to replenish the lighthouse's provisions. To the captain's surprise, there was no sign of the keepers, even though the lighthouse's lamp was still functioning. This detail, seemingly mundane, raises the first enigma – how could the light remain operational without the keepers' presence, especially considering that the oil supply had run low and a fresh supply was delivered? The official investigation, conducted by the Northern Lighthouse Board, concluded that the keepers had likely fallen victim to a storm, their bodies swept away by the unforgiving sea. However, this explanation, while plausible, fails to address several key inconsistencies. .

The absence of any signs of struggle, the absence of bodies despite the thorough search efforts, and the meticulously maintained condition of the lighthouse, including the fully wound clock, present a perplexing scenario that defies a simple explanation. The keepers had vanished without a trace, leaving behind no clues, no messages, and no indication of a struggle. This lack of evidence casts a long shadow of doubt on the storm theory, suggesting a more sinister and mysterious explanation for their disappearance.

The isolation of Eilean Mor, coupled with the eerie silence surrounding the incident, has fueled a vibrant tapestry of conspiracy theories. Some suggest that the keepers were abducted by a passing ship, perhaps a vessel engaged in smuggling or illicit activities. Others speculate on the possibility of foul play, perhaps a violent confrontation that resulted in the silencing of the keepers. The presence of a hidden cache of whiskey, discovered later, further complicates the narrative, leading some to believe that the keepers may have been caught in a dangerous game with illicit alcohol smugglers, their fate sealed in a desperate attempt to protect their secret.

The enduring allure of the Eilean Mor mystery lies in its tantalizing ambiguity. There is no definitive answer, no smoking gun, no clear resolution. The whispers of the sea, the silence of the island, and the ghostly absence of the keepers continue to echo through the annals of time, beckoning us to piece together the fragments of this baffling puzzle. The lack of conclusive evidence has fostered an atmosphere of intrigue, allowing imagination and speculation to run wild. The mystery of the Eilean Mor lighthouse remains, a haunting testament to the power of the unknown and the enduring fascination we have with the inexplicable. .

.

Chapter 9: The Weather Factor

Analysis of weather conditions during the disappearance

The weather surrounding the disappearance of the three lighthouse keepers on Eilean Mor in 1900 remains an enigma, a significant factor that, while not offering a conclusive explanation, contributes to the mystery's enduring allure. The official accounts, primarily based on the logbook found on the island, paint a picture of a storm on December 15th, but with notable inconsistencies and a lack of detail that leaves room for speculation. .

The logbook entry, stark in its brevity, mentions "a heavy gale" and the presence of "a tremendous sea. " However, the record lacks specifics regarding wind speed, wave height, and the duration of the storm, crucial data for any meteorological analysis. Additionally, the absence of any further details about the storm's intensity, including observations of damage or specific events, is striking. This lack of information leaves room for doubt about the actual severity of the storm and its true impact on the lighthouse.

The initial investigations, hampered by the island's remoteness, focused primarily on the possibility of a maritime disaster caused by the reported storm. The sea's roughness, even if exaggerated by the logbook's brevity, could certainly have posed a danger, especially for venturing out in a small boat. Yet, there are aspects of the story that contradict this simple explanation.

The lighthouse keepers, experienced mariners, were accustomed to navigating rough seas. The presence of the fully functional lantern and the untouched state of the lighthouse itself strongly suggest that the keepers were not caught unprepared by the storm. Furthermore, the lack of any wreckage from their boat near the island casts doubt on the notion of a seafaring accident, adding to the mystery surrounding their disappearance.

Weather records from the nearby mainland, crucial for understanding the regional meteorological conditions, reveal a different picture. While a storm did indeed pass through the area on December 15th, it was classified as moderate, not the "heavy gale" mentioned in the logbook. This disparity highlights the difficulty in relying solely on the logbook for accurate information about the weather, especially considering its brevity and the potential for exaggeration or misinterpretation. .

It's essential to consider the psychological impact of isolation and the unusual circumstances of the event. The three keepers were alone on a remote island with limited communication with the mainland. They may have been subject to heightened anxiety and perceived the storm as more severe than it actually was, potentially leading to misjudgments and actions driven by fear. .

Moreover, the weather reports from the mainland provide valuable insights into the potential causes of the disappearance. They suggest that the storm may have been localized, perhaps even a rogue wave that impacted the island in a particularly intense and destructive way. The possibility of a sudden, unpredictable event, rather than a prolonged storm, could explain the lack of wreckage and the lack of detailed information in the logbook.

While the official reports highlight a storm on December 15th, the lack of detail and inconsistencies raise questions about its actual severity. The weather records from the mainland, contrasting with the logbook's claims, introduce the possibility of a localized, unpredictable event, adding another layer of intrigue to the enigma. The weather, therefore, acts as a catalyst for speculation, fueling the mystery of the keepers' disappearance and leaving a lingering sense of uncertainty about the true events that unfolded on Eilean Mor that fateful December. .

.

The role of storms and the lighthouse's vulnerability

The howling wind whips around the granite monolith of Eilean Mor Lighthouse, a fury unleashed from the depths of the North Atlantic. It's not merely a backdrop; it's an antagonist, a force that tests the very essence of the lighthouse's existence. The sea, normally a source of life and sustenance, transforms into a monstrous entity, spitting waves that thunder against the lighthouse's foundations. Its vulnerability lies not just in its exposed location, but in the way the storm becomes an insidious assailant, chipping away at the lighthouse's strength with every crashing wave.

The very structure of Eilean Mor, seemingly impregnable, is subject to the relentless barrage of the elements. Its unforgiving environment becomes a silent, invisible enemy, slowly eroding the stone, the iron, the very fabric of the lighthouse. The relentless battering, a constant assault on the lighthouse's integrity, is not merely a physical threat; it's a psychological one, a silent pressure that weighs upon the souls of the men who stand watch. This is a vulnerability that is often overlooked, a quiet erosion that can weaken the will of even the most hardened soul.

The storms that rage around Eilean Mor are more than just meteorological events; they are harbingers of isolation and danger. The tempestuous weather transforms the lighthouse into a prison, cutting off its inhabitants from the mainland, rendering them utterly reliant on the lighthouse's own defenses. The lighthouse keepers, trapped within its walls, become pawns in a game of survival, their fate intertwined with the lighthouse's resilience against the wrath of the sea. .

Beyond the physical vulnerability, the storms also highlight the fragility of the human spirit. The men stationed at Eilean Mor are not merely keepers of the light; they are guardians against the darkness of the storm, tasked with maintaining the fragile thread of hope that keeps the ships from disaster. The unrelenting nature of the storms, their ability to envelop the lighthouse in a suffocating blanket of fog and rain, can create a sense of despair that burrows into the heart, a feeling of insignificance against the vast power of nature.

The lighthouse's vulnerability in the face of the storm isn't just structural; it's a testament to the inherent fragility of human existence. The keepers, isolated, facing down the fury of the sea, are a stark reminder that nature holds the ultimate power, capable of extinguishing even the strongest of lights. This is not simply a lighthouse; it's a symbol of human resilience, a beacon against the encroaching darkness, but it is also a testament to the ever-present possibility of extinction, a poignant reminder of our vulnerability in the face of the untamed wild.

The storm is not just an element; it's an integral part of the narrative. Its unrelenting presence, its ability to transform the lighthouse into a besieged fortress, becomes a metaphor for the unseen forces that can shape our lives, the unpredictable twists of fate that can challenge even the strongest of wills. The vulnerability of the lighthouse, its struggle to endure the storm's relentless assault, echoes the struggle of the human spirit, its constant battle against the elements, both internal and external.

Eilean Mor Lighthouse stands as a testament to the power of nature, a reminder of the ceaseless struggle between human ambition and the untamed forces of the world. The storms, in their relentless assault, expose the fragility of the lighthouse, its vulnerability to the whims of the sea. They become a catalyst for the narrative, highlighting the isolation, the fear, the relentless pressure that the keepers endure, the very essence of their struggle to stay alive against the relentless onslaught of the storm. .

Chapter 10: The Sea's Fury

The treacherous nature of the surrounding waters

The treacherous nature of the waters surrounding Eilean Mòr Lighthouse is a constant, ever-present threat, woven into the very fabric of the story of the vanishing keepers. The North Atlantic, a vast and unforgiving ocean, crashes relentlessly against the jagged, unforgiving coastline of the Outer Hebrides. Here, the sea is not a tranquil haven, but a wild, capricious force, capable of unleashing its fury with little warning. The sheer scale of the ocean itself, with its seemingly boundless expanse and depths that plunge into the unknown, instills a sense of awe and trepidation. This is not the gentle, predictable sea of calmer shores; here, currents shift and churn, forming unpredictable eddies and whirlpools that can swallow a ship whole. .

The currents around Eilean Mòr are particularly treacherous, a maelstrom of conflicting forces that can render even the most experienced mariner helpless. The Gulf Stream, a warm current flowing north from the tropics, meets the colder waters of the North Atlantic, creating a chaotic interplay of forces that can quickly turn calm seas into a raging tempest. The narrow, treacherous sound that separates the island from the mainland further intensifies these currents, creating a funnel effect that amplifies their power. The strong tidal flows, surging in and out with the rhythm of the moon, further add to the instability, making navigation a perilous exercise. .

Even on seemingly calm days, the unpredictable nature of the sea can reveal itself in a moment. Dense fogs, rolling in from the west, can blanket the island in a shroud of impenetrable mist, rendering landmarks invisible and obscuring even the nearby mainland. These fogs, clinging stubbornly to the cold, damp air, are not merely a nuisance; they can become a death sentence, disorienting ships and blinding them to the looming dangers of the coastline. Waves, seemingly innocuous at first, can swell into towering, thunderous behemoths driven by strong winds that howl across the exposed landscape. The relentless pounding of these waves against the rocky shores, a constant drumbeat that echoes across the island, speaks of the raw, untamed power of the ocean.

The sea around Eilean Mòr is not just treacherous, it is unforgiving. It offers no respite, no sanctuary from its relentless assault. The frigid waters, a chilling embrace that can numb the body and steal the breath, hold a constant threat of hypothermia. The treacherous currents, ever-shifting and unpredictable, can drag a man down into their depths, never to be seen again. The rocky coastline, a jagged, unforgiving barrier against the sea's fury, is a testament to the relentless power of the waves, a constant reminder of the dangers that lurk just beyond the lighthouse's lonely gaze. .

The sea around Eilean Mòr is a living entity, a force of nature to be respected and feared. It is a constant presence, a brooding, unpredictable entity that dictates the lives of those who dare to live on its shores. The story of the vanishing keepers is a chilling testament to the power of the sea, a story that forever links the fate of men to the unforgiving embrace of the ocean. . .

Accounts of other accidents and disappearances

The eerie vanishing of the three keepers from Eilean Mor Lighthouse in 1900 is a chilling tale, a chilling reminder of the relentless power of the sea and the isolation of those who brave its fury. Yet, it is not a singular event. The annals of maritime history are filled with stories of disappearances, accidents, and the sea's seemingly inexplicable wrath. These accounts, though disparate in detail, resonate with the same unsettling questions that haunt Eilean Mor: what happened? Where did they go? What unseen forces could claim lives and vanish without a trace? .

A haunting echo of Eilean Mor is found in the disappearance of the SV "Mary Celeste," a 19th-century merchant vessel found adrift and seemingly deserted in 1872. Though multiple theories have been proposed, including mutiny, piracy, and even a giant squid attack, no definitive explanation has been found for the vessel's abandonment. The crew's disappearance, like that of the Eilean Mor keepers, remains a chilling mystery, leaving behind a lingering sense of unease and unanswered questions. .

The desolate shores of the Island of St. Kilda in the Outer Hebrides, not far from Eilean Mor, hold a harrowing tale of shipwreck. The "Iolaire," a British transport ship, carrying home returning World War I soldiers, struck the rocks near the island in 1919, claiming the lives of over 200 men. The tragedy, exacerbated by a blinding snowstorm and thick fog, serves as a stark reminder of the treacherous nature of the seas surrounding the islands, and the chilling vulnerability of those who venture out into their unpredictable fury. .

The "Titanic," a symbol of human ambition and technological prowess, met its tragic end in the icy waters of the North Atlantic in 1912, a chilling reminder of the sea's indifference to human hubris. The sinking, fueled by negligence and the ship's inadequate safety measures, claimed over 1,500 lives. While the tragedy of the Titanic is not a disappearance, it reflects a profound lack of preparedness and a disregard for the sea's power, much like the tragic case of the "MV Derbyshire," a bulk carrier that vanished without a trace during a typhoon in 1980. The "Derbyshire," thought to be the largest vessel ever to disappear at sea, leaving behind no survivors, serves as a stark reminder of the sea's capability to engulf even the most modern and seemingly invulnerable ships.

The sea, a source of life and beauty, can also be a formidable adversary. These accounts, alongside the enigma of Eilean Mor, underscore the power of the unknown and the unsettling nature of the ocean's mysteries. They leave a lasting impression, a lingering question of what else lies beneath the surface, hidden from our view, waiting to reveal its secrets in a moment of terrifying power.

Chapter 11: Supernatural Beliefs

Local legends and folklore related to the lighthouse

The Eilean Mor lighthouse, perched precariously on the windswept island of Eilean Mor off the coast of Scotland, has long been shrouded in a misty veil of local lore and legend. This imposing sentinel, a beacon of hope in the treacherous waters, has inspired whispers of the supernatural and tales of eerie happenings, woven through the fabric of local folklore. The island itself, with its rugged terrain and isolated setting, provided fertile ground for these narratives. Locals spoke of the island's spectral inhabitants, of the lingering presence of ancient spirits that roamed the desolate landscape. The lighthouse, with its stark white facade and the hypnotic rhythm of its beam cutting through the darkness, became a focal point for these whispers. .

The island's past was rife with stories of shipwrecks and tragedy, with sailors lost to the unforgiving seas. These tales of maritime disaster seeped into the fabric of the island's folklore, shaping the perception of Eilean Mor as a place of peril and haunting echoes. It was whispered that the souls of those lost at sea clung to the shores of Eilean Mor, their cries carried on the wind, their presence felt in the chill that seemed to pervade the island. .

One of the most persistent legends surrounding the lighthouse concerned the "Grey Man of Eilean Mor." This mysterious figure, cloaked in a mist-like grey, was said to appear at the lighthouse, a harbinger of misfortune. The locals believed that the Grey Man was a spectral guardian, a protector of the island who warned of impending danger. His ghostly form, often seen in the swirling mists, was said to be a sign of impending storms or shipwrecks. It was believed that those who encountered the Grey Man were destined to face misfortune, their fate sealed by the apparition. This spectral presence, with its ominous aura, added another layer of mystique to the already haunted air surrounding the lighthouse. .

Tales of the Grey Man were often intertwined with stories of "The Fog of Eilean Mor," a dense, impenetrable mist that was said to descend upon the island without warning, blanketing it in an eerie silence. This fog, considered a harbinger of tragedy, was believed to be a physical manifestation of the island's supernatural aura. It was said that the fog could trap the unwary, leading them astray and into the unforgiving embrace of the sea. This thick, enigmatic mist, with its otherworldly connotations, contributed to the air of mystery and dread that enveloped Eilean Mor. .

The Eilean Mor lighthouse itself, a towering sentinel against the tempestuous sea, became a symbol of isolation and vulnerability. It stood as a testament to the power of the sea, a beacon of warning to those who dared venture near its shores. The lighthouse, with its solitary keepers, was perceived as a place cut off from the world, a place where the veil between the mortal and the supernatural was thin. Stories of the lighthouse keepers, disappearing into the night, leaving behind only a chilling emptiness, fueled the local lore. The isolation of the lighthouse, its remote location, contributed to the sense of mystery and fueled the imaginations of those who lived in the surrounding communities. .

The Eilean Mor lighthouse became a magnet for those who sought the extraordinary, attracting those who believed in the supernatural and sought to experience the island's enigmatic energy. These seekers, drawn to the mystery and the tales of the Grey Man and the Fog of Eilean Mor, added their own interpretations to the local lore, weaving their experiences into the tapestry of the island's legend. The stories of Eilean Mor and its lighthouse, passed down through generations, became a part of the island's identity, shaping the perception of the lighthouse as a place of mystery and wonder, a place where the supernatural intermingled with the natural world. .

The lighthouse, a beacon of light against the darkness, also became a symbol of hope, a reminder of humanity's enduring spirit in the face of the unknown. It stood as a testament to the resilience of the human spirit, its unwavering presence a source of comfort in the face of the island's supernatural lore. However, despite the stories, despite the lingering tales of the Grey Man and the fog that enveloped the island, the lighthouse remained a powerful symbol of hope, a guiding light in the darkness, a reminder that even in the most isolated of places, humanity and the natural world can coexist. The Eilean Mor lighthouse, a sentinel against the storms, a beacon against the darkness, continues to stand as a testament to the power of human ingenuity, its ghostly stories weaving themselves into the fabric of the island's legend. .

.

Theories of ghostly hauntings or other paranormal phenomena

The disappearance of the three lighthouse keepers from Eilean Mor in 1900, a remote island off the coast of Scotland, has fueled speculation about the possibility of paranormal forces at play. The lack of any concrete evidence of foul play or external threats has led many to explore the ethereal realm for answers. The haunting of the lighthouse, a solitary sentinel against the harsh Atlantic, seems woven into the very fabric of the island's history, leaving behind a chilling legacy of unexplained events. .

One prevailing theory revolves around the idea of residual hauntings, where the spirits of the missing keepers are trapped on the island, unable to find peace. Their tragic fate, the sudden and mysterious disappearance, creates a powerful energy that lingers, manifesting as unexplained occurrences. The lighthouse itself, a silent witness to their ordeal, acts as a conduit for this trapped energy, amplifying their residual presence. .

The psychometric effect is another intriguing possibility. The lighthouse, imbued with the memories of the keepers, their routines, and their final moments, acts as a focal point for psychic energy. The objects within the lighthouse, like the clocks that stopped at the moment of their disappearance, become repositories of this energy, potentially triggering psychic experiences in those who come into contact with them. Those visiting the lighthouse, vulnerable to these residual energies, might perceive them as ghostly apparitions or unexplained sounds.

There is also the intriguing concept of environmental anomalies, where the location itself contributes to the paranormal phenomena. Eilean Mor, isolated and shrouded in mist, is a place where the boundaries between reality and the supernatural blur. The harsh weather, the swirling fog, and the constant pounding of the waves against the island's cliffs all contribute to a sense of unease, making it easier to believe in the inexplicable. This heightened sense of vulnerability, coupled with the island's isolation and the tragic history of the lighthouse, could amplify any paranormal experiences.

Then there is the possibility of external malevolent entities, where the hauntings are not directly tied to the missing keepers but to an independent, malevolent force. This entity, attracted to the island's isolation and the lingering energy of the missing keepers, exploits the lighthouse as a gateway into the human world. This theory, however, struggles to explain the lack of evidence of any other victims or unexplained phenomena outside the lighthouse's walls.

It's important to note that the theories surrounding the Eilean Mor disappearances are often intertwined, creating a complex tapestry of possibilities. Perhaps the island's isolation, the tragic fate of the keepers, and the lighthouse's haunted legacy all contribute to an atmosphere that attracts paranormal activity, making it difficult to pinpoint any single cause.

The enduring mystery of the Eilean Mor lighthouse continues to fascinate, prompting endless speculation and a deep sense of unease. Whether it's the trapped souls of the missing keepers or a malevolent entity, the lighthouse stands as a testament to the power of the unknown, a place where the boundaries between reality and the supernatural are forever blurred. The whispers of the past, carried on the wind and echoing through the corridors of the lighthouse, continue to draw those seeking answers, leaving them with more questions than answers, and a chilling reminder of the enduring mystery of Eilean Mor.

Chapter 12: The Unsolved Enigma

The ongoing fascination with the case

The Eilean Mor lighthouse, a sentinel against the tempestuous North Atlantic, stands as a silent monument to a mystery that has captivated the world for over a century. The vanishing of Thomas Marshall, James Ducat, and Donald MacArthur, the lighthouse keepers, in 1900, has become a touchstone of the uncanny, a haunting reminder of the vast, unknowable forces that can engulf even the most steadfast human presence. This enduring fascination with the Eilean Mor case transcends mere morbid curiosity; it taps into primal anxieties about isolation, the unpredictable nature of the natural world, and the fragility of human existence in the face of the unknown.

The circumstances of the disappearance, shrouded in a veil of conflicting evidence and unanswered questions, fuel a constant hunger for explanation. The eerie emptiness of the lighthouse, the meticulously maintained machinery, the untouched meal prepared for the missing men, and the chillingly incomplete logbook all contribute to a narrative that tantalizes and unsettles. The absence of any clear signs of struggle or forced departure suggests a disappearance far more sinister than a simple escape or an act of foul play. This ambiguity, this tantalizing lack of closure, is what sustains the Eilean Mor enigma.

The isolation of Eilean Mor itself plays a critical role in the enduring allure of the case. Perched precariously on a desolate rock amidst the tumultuous Atlantic, the lighthouse becomes a microcosm of human vulnerability, a beacon of civilization standing against the relentless forces of nature. The very isolation that allowed the keepers to maintain the vital service of the lighthouse also rendered them vulnerable, leaving them at the mercy of whatever unseen forces claimed them. This stark contrast between the vital importance of the lighthouse and the fragility of its human protectors creates a sense of both awe and dread, making the Eilean Mor mystery a potent allegory for the inherent precariousness of human life.

The Eilean Mor lighthouse has become a symbolic touchstone for our collective anxieties about the unknown. It stands as a reminder that even in the most advanced age of science and technology, the world remains a place of unsettling mysteries. The case continues to inspire countless books, documentaries, and works of fiction, each seeking to unravel the puzzle, to shed light on the darkness that engulfed the lighthouse keepers. Yet, despite the countless theories and attempts at reconstruction, the truth remains elusive, a tantalizing enigma that continues to captivate our imaginations.

The fascination with the Eilean Mor lighthouse case speaks to a deeper human need to comprehend the inexplicable, to find order in the face of chaos. It is a testament to our enduring fascination with the unknown, our drive to confront the unsettling truth that there are forces in the universe that may forever remain beyond our understanding. The case of the vanished keepers serves as a potent reminder of the vastness and unpredictability of the world, a world where even the most resolute human endeavor can be swallowed by the enigmatic forces that surround us.

The Eilean Mor lighthouse, a silent sentinel against the relentless Atlantic, continues to beckon with its unanswered questions. Its mystery transcends time, reminding us that the unknown remains an enduring force, shaping our fears, fueling our curiosity, and ultimately defining our shared human experience. The case of the vanished keepers serves as a potent reminder of the limits of human knowledge, a stark reminder that even in the face of scientific progress, the world continues to hold secrets that may forever remain beyond our grasp. .

.

The enduring mystery of the missing keepers

The Eilean Mor lighthouse, perched on a desolate rock island off the coast of Scotland, stands as a silent sentinel to a haunting enigma: the vanishing of its keepers in 1900. The disappearance of James Ducat, Thomas Marshall, and Donald MacArthur, the lighthouse's keepers, remains a chilling mystery that continues to captivate and baffle investigators, historians, and amateur sleuths alike. The circumstances of their disappearance, shrouded in a veil of isolation and unanswered questions, have cemented their story in the annals of unsolved mysteries, a tale whispered among mariners and echoed through the passage of time.

The chilling backdrop of the disappearance, a desolate and unforgiving island battered by harsh weather and swirling seas, adds a layer of unease to the story. Eilean Mor, Gaelic for "Big Island," was a remote outpost, accessible only by boat and subject to the whims of the unpredictable North Atlantic. The isolation of the lighthouse, a stark reminder of the keepers' vulnerability, serves as a poignant symbol of their vulnerability. Their routine, a solitary existence punctuated by the rhythmic pulse of the lighthouse beam, was abruptly shattered by an inexplicable event.

The absence of a clear motive for the disappearance, coupled with the lack of any obvious signs of struggle or foul play, deepens the enigma. No evidence of a forced departure, no indication of a struggle, and no trace of any of the keepers' belongings was found. The absence of any signs of a struggle, a robbery, or even a suicide suggests an unsettlingly unnatural and unexplained vanishing. The fact that their clockwork machinery was meticulously wound and ready for operation adds to the mystery, suggesting the keepers didn't abandon their post voluntarily, adding a chilling layer to the puzzle.

The official investigation, hampered by the remoteness of the island and the lack of evidence, was inconclusive. The initial theories, ranging from a maritime disaster to foul play, were quickly debunked, leaving the mystery unsolved. The absence of a definitive answer, the enigma of the missing keepers, has endured, turning the lighthouse into a silent monument to an unsolved mystery.

Over a century later, the story of the missing keepers continues to be scrutinized, debated, and dissected. Each new theory, each fresh interpretation of the available evidence, only serves to deepen the intrigue surrounding the Eilean Mor lighthouse. The enduring mystery, a haunting testament to the power of the unknown, continues to capture the imaginations of those who dare to venture into the heart of the enigma. It is a story whispered across generations, a story that speaks to the primal fear of the unknown, and a story that continues to echo through the solitude of the remote Scottish island. The Eilean Mor lighthouse, with its flickering beam cutting through the night, stands as a silent reminder of the enduring mystery of the vanished keepers, a testament to the chilling power of the unexplained.

.

Lessons learned for lighthouse safety and communication

The chilling tale of the Eilean Mor Lighthouse, a remote sentinel perched on the rugged Scottish coast, offers a stark reminder of the critical need for robust safety protocols and communication systems in maritime operations. While the mystery surrounding the disappearance of the three keepers in 1900 remains unsolved, the tragic incident lays bare the vulnerability of isolated lighthouses and the dangers inherent in their operation. .

The lack of regular communication, underscored by the absence of any distress calls from the keepers, highlights the vital importance of establishing reliable and consistent channels for contact. In the early 20th century, the reliance on rudimentary methods like Morse code and semaphore flags, susceptible to weather disruptions and limited range, proved insufficient for maintaining a lifeline with isolated stations like Eilean Mor. .

The incident underscores the urgent need for advanced technologies that can overcome geographical and environmental barriers. Satellite communication, with its global reach and resistance to weather interference, would have undoubtedly transformed the situation. Real-time monitoring systems could have detected any anomalies, be it equipment failure, weather events, or unusual activity.

Moreover, the investigation revealed a disturbing lack of standardized procedures for lighthouse operations and the absence of a comprehensive emergency plan. This lapse in protocols was a contributing factor to the delayed response and the difficulty in coordinating search and rescue efforts. The Eilean Mor case necessitates the implementation of rigorous training programs for lighthouse keepers, covering not just technical aspects of operation but also crisis management, emergency response, and search and rescue procedures.

Another critical lesson learned revolves around the importance of regular inspections and maintenance. The investigation revealed that the lighthouse equipment had malfunctioned, including a broken foghorn, raising concerns about the frequency of maintenance visits and the effectiveness of the inspection protocols. Implementing a strict schedule for routine checks and preventive maintenance, coupled with advanced monitoring systems to detect equipment failures remotely, would have significantly mitigated the risk of such an incident.

The Eilean Mor tragedy serves as a stark reminder of the inherent dangers associated with remote maritime operations. The isolation, unpredictable weather conditions, and reliance on human vigilance demand robust safety protocols, advanced communication systems, and a culture of continuous improvement. This tragic incident, though shrouded in mystery, stands as a testament to the need for constant vigilance and the relentless pursuit of safety in all maritime endeavors. .

.